TABLE OF CONTENTS

SPONGE PATROL................1

KRABBY HEROES..............10

FINDERS KEEPERS............18

ZAP! PART I....................27

WHALE OF A TALE...............38

SQUIDWARD'S REVENGE......50

ZAP! PART II....................55

OH, PICKLE!....................65

WUMBORAMA..................72

ZAP! PART III..................79

FISH JAR.......................89

TINY TOWN....................95

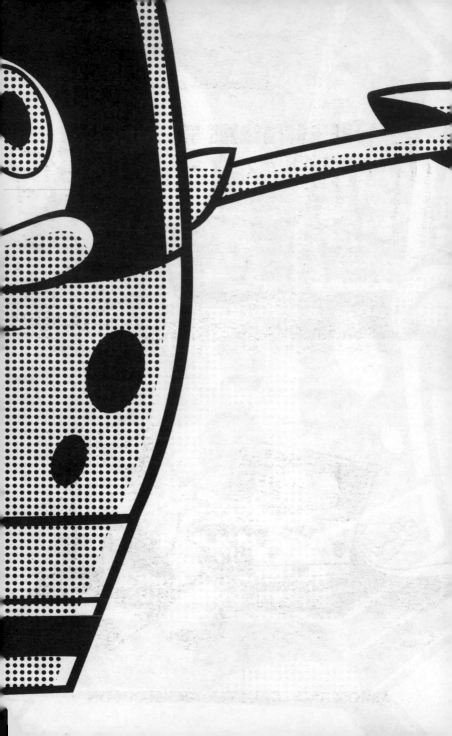

THE ADVENTURES OF

MAN SPONGE AND BOY PATRICK

IN WHAT WERE YOU SHRINKING?

BY DAVID LEWMAN | ILLUSTRATED BY THE ARTIFACT GROUP

SIMON AND SCHUSTER/NICKELODEON

Based on the TV series *SpongeBob SquarePants*™ created by Stephen Hillenburg as seen on Nickelodeon™

SIMON AND SCHUSTER
First published in Great Britain in 2012 by Simon & Schuster UK
1st Floor, 222 Gray's Inn Road, London WC1X 8HB
A CBS Company

Originally published in the USA in 2011 by Simon Spotlight, an imprint of Simon & Schuster Children's Division, New York.
© 2012 Viacom International Inc. All rights reserved.
NICKELODEON, SpongeBob SquarePants, and all related titles, logos and characters are trademarks of Viacom International Inc.
Created by Stephen Hillenburg.

A CIP catalogue record for this book is available from the British Library

ISBN 978-0-85707-337-2

Printed and bound by CPI Group (UK) Ltd, Croydon, CR0 4YY

1 3 5 7 9 10 8 6 4 2

Designed by Victor Joseph Ochoa

SPONGE PATROL

It was a quiet day in Bikini Bottom, and SpongeBob and Patrick were eager for an adventure.

"I think it's time, Patrick," SpongeBob told his best friend seriously.

"Time for what?" Patrick asked.

"For some superhero action!" SpongeBob cried out.

Five seconds later, Man Sponge and Boy Patrick marched through downtown Bikini Bottom on their daily rounds. The two super-heroes were eager to help anyone in trouble.

"Keep a sharp eye out for citizens in need," Man Sponge reminded Boy Patrick.

"Aye-aye, Man Sponge," Boy Patrick answered, saluting.

Suddenly, Man Sponge pointed. "Look, Boy Patrick! A person in distress!"

Boy Patrick peered in the direction Man Sponge was pointing. "You mean that rubbish bin? You're right! It needs to be emptied!"

"No, I mean the lady next to the rubbish bin!" Man Sponge explained. "She obviously wants to cross the street, but she can't get through the villainous traffic without the aid of . . . MAN SPONGE AND . . ."

"BOY PATRICK!" added Boy Patrick. Together they rushed over to the elderly woman, picked her up, and dashed across the street!

When they reached the opposite side of
the busy avenue, they set the lady down. "No
need to thank us, ma'am!" Man Sponge
said, smiling. "It's all in a day's work for Man
Sponge . . ."

"And Boy Patrick!"

The two of them ran off. The woman
looked puzzled. "But I didn't *want* to cross
the street," she said. "My bus stops on the
other side."

By that time, Man Sponge had already moved on to another citizen in need. "Boy Patrick, if I'm not mistaken—and I never am—that young fellow there is being attacked by a vicious creature!"

Without a second's hesitation, the two superheroes sprinted over and got between the beast and the boy. "Run, lad!" shouted

Man Sponge. "We'll handle the monster!"

The boy looked confused. "What monster?"

Man Sponge pointed at the fearsome beast. "That monster right there!"

The boy looked insulted. "That's not a monster! That's my pet worm, Crawler. I'm taking him for a walk. Come on, boy."

The worm happily followed its owner. Boy Patrick looked concerned. "I don't like this,

Man Sponge. It's like that monster has the kid under some kind of mind-control ray!"

"There's no time to think about that!" Man Sponge cried. "We've got to save Pearl from the evil Teenage Guy!"

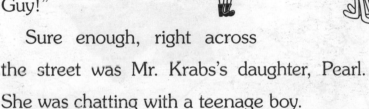

Sure enough, right across the street was Mr. Krabs's daughter, Pearl. She was chatting with a teenage boy.

"Um, Pearl," he asked nervously. "Do you think maybe you might like to, um, go with me to the, um, dance next—"

"HOLD IT RIGHT THERE, TEENAGE GUY!" Man Sponge bellowed. "That fair, young damsel is under the constant protection of Man Sponge . . ."

"And Boy Patrick!" chimed in Boy Patrick.

Pearl looked annoyed. Derek had finally gotten up the nerve to ask her to the dance, and then these two come barging in! "Shouldn't you be at work?" she snapped.

Man Sponge looked at his watch and gasped. "Gadzooks!" he cried. "The lass is right! I'm due at the Krusty Krab, where I toil under the guise of my mild-mannered secret identity, SpongeBob SquarePants!" He dashed off to work.

Derek watched him go. "You know, it's not much of a secret identity if you announce it to everyone," he said.

He and Pearl stood there awkwardly with Patrick for a minute. "So," Patrick asked, "you two want to get a milk shake?"

KRABBY HEROES

SpongeBob zipped through the dining room of the Krusty Krab. "Hi, Squidward! It's just me, SpongeBob, ready for work!"

"What a surprise," Squidward said dryly. SpongeBob hurried into the kitchen and got to work cooking Krabby Patties. The only thing he loved more than patrolling Bikini Bottom as Man Sponge was his wonderful job at the Krusty Krab.

Out front, Mermaidman burst into the dining room. "Through the double doors, away!" he cried.

His faithful sidekick, Barnacleboy, followed him into the restaurant. "I told you," he said. "I'm not hungry, Mermaidman."

Shocked, Mermaidman whipped around to face his loyal assistant. "Nonsense, Barnacleboy!" he insisted. "We've got to keep up our strength for the fight against . . . *EEEEEEEVVVIIIIIIL!*"

Barnacleboy looked around the fast-food restaurant. "What a dive," he muttered.

"To the register, away!" Mermaidman announced as he ran toward Squidward to place his order.

"Can I help you?" asked Squidward, sounding as if the last thing he wanted to do was help anyone.

Mermaidman studied the menu hanging on the wall above Squidward's head. "A double Krabby Patty and Coral Bits for me," he said. "And a Silly Meal for the lad," he added, pointing his thumb toward Barnacleboy.

"It's not for the toy!" Barnacleboy explained, feeling a little embarrassed. "I just gotta fit in the tights." Squidward could not have cared less. "Whatever," he said. "Five dollars, please."

"You got it, Bucky!" Mermaidman said. He rummaged around in his coin purse and pulled out a button. "Will this cover it?"

"No," Squidward said, looking disgusted.

Barnacleboy leaned in close to Squidward. "Listen, big nose," he said, glaring. "That guy's been saving your butt since before you were born. Don't you have a living-legend discount or something?"

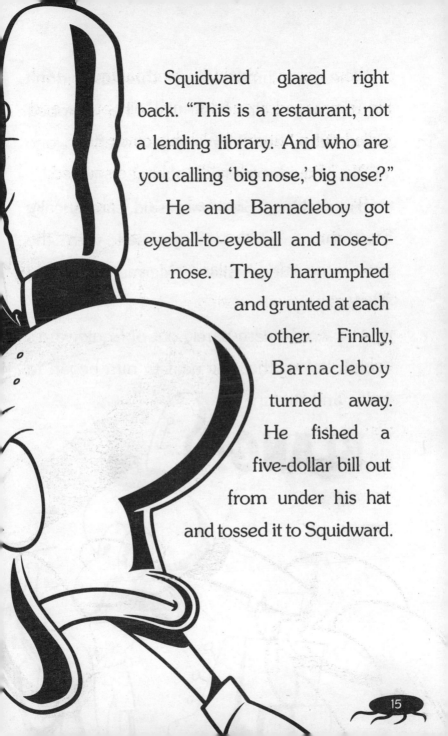

Squidward glared right back. "This is a restaurant, not a lending library. And who are you calling 'big nose,' big nose?"

He and Barnacleboy got eyeball-to-eyeball and nose-to-nose. They harrumphed and grunted at each other. Finally, Barnacleboy turned away. He fished a five-dollar bill out from under his hat and tossed it to Squidward.

"The next time danger threatens, don't expect any help from us!" he snapped. Barnacleboy and Mermaidman went to one of the dining tables to sit down.

"I'm shaking," Squidward said, sarcastically. Then he snorted, unimpressed with the two aging superheroes. "Mermaidman and Barnacleboy—"

The words were barely out of Squidward's mouth before the wall next to him began to bulge and stretch.

BLANG!

SpongeBob burst through the wall into the dining area.

"MERMAIDMAN AND BARNACLEBOY!" he said loudly, his voice trembling with excitement. "MUST . . . GET . . . AUTOGRAPH!"

FINDERS KEEPERS

Without a moment to lose, SpongeBob sprang into action. He shot his right arm across the room and grabbed a pen from a customer's pocket. He stretched his left arm out a window and snatched a piece of paper floating by. Now he was ready!

At their table, Mermaidman and Barnacleboy waited for their food. "If you want to grow up strong

like me," Mermaidman said, smiling, "you've gotta make room for seconds." He unfastened his bell, and his stomach popped out.

"Here comes our waiter!" he added.

But it was no waiter. It was SpongeBob, running toward their table, vibrating with anticipation.

AUTOOGRAAAPH!"

he cried.

Barnacleboy looked alarmed. "Holy sea cow! It's that sponge kid!"

"Quick, lad!" Mermaidman said. "To the Invisible Boatmobile! Awaaay!"

Mermaidman leaped up. His trousers fell down, revealing his polka-dot boxer shorts. He pulled them up and ran out of the Krusty Krab, followed by Barnacleboy.

Once outside, they stared at the crowded parking lot. "Where'd we park?" Barnacleboy asked.

"Uhhh . . . ," Mermaidman said, trying hard to remember.

Back inside the Krusty
Krab, SpongeBob reached
their table, overwhelmed.

"Can I have your autograph? Can I have
your autograph?" he chattered. Then he
realized his two favourite superheroes weren't
there. "They're gone!"

Looking around to see where they went,
SpongeBob spotted something on the floor
and gasped. "Mermaidman's belt!"

Outside, Mermaidman and Barnacleboy were still searching for their boat. Then Mermaidman got an idea. "We'll find it with the Invisible Boat Alarm!"

He pulled an invisible remote control out of his pocket and pressed a button.

CHIRP, CHIRP!

CHIRP, CHIRP!

In a nearby parking place, the Invisible Boatmobile flashed into view, becoming visible for just a second.

Mermaidman pointed gleefully. "There she is!" He and Barnacleboy jumped, flying through the air, toward the Invisible Boatmobile.

Unfortunately, Barnacleboy landed right on the stick shift.

"YEOWWWCH!"

he cried.

"I told you we should have gotten the automatic!"

23

SpongeBob burst out of the Krusty Krab's front doors carrying Mermaidman's belt. "Hey, guys! Wait up! I've got something for you!"

But all Mermaidman and Barnacleboy saw was an overeager fan trying to get an autograph.

"Floor it!" Barnacleboy yelled.

Mermaidman hit the gas, and the invisible engine roared to life. Flames shot out the back of the boat, and the two superheroes sped off into the distance.

"You forgot your belt!" SpongeBob called.

But it was no use. The superheroes were gone.

ZAP!

PART I

SpongeBob looked at the belt and his eyes got big with wonder.

"Mermaidman's secret utility belt!" he said. "The emblem of submersible justice. For sixty-five years this belt has helped prevent the fall of nations. And trousers. I can't believe I'm actually holding it in my hands."

SpongeBob started thinking about all the amazing Mermaidman and Barnacleboy adventures that featured the secret utility belt. There was one in particular that he remembered well. . . .

Mermaidman and Barnacleboy were surrounded by bad guys—the Dirty Bubble, Man Ray, Jumbo Shrimp, the Atomic Flounder. . . .

"We're in a pickle this time, Barnacleboy!" cried Mermaidman.

"Yep, we're in a jam for sure," agreed Barnacleboy.

Then a voice rang out. "Pickles taste terrible with jam!"

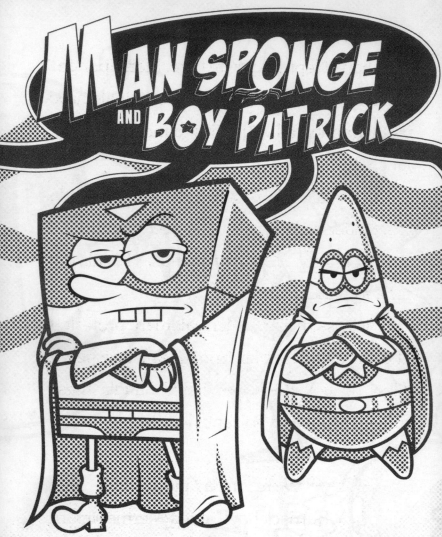

MAN SPONGE
AND BOY PATRICK

It was Man Sponge! And his faithful sidekick, Boy Patrick! They had arrived to help Mermaidman and Barnacleboy defeat the villains!

"Thank Neptune you're here, Man Sponge!" gushed Mermaidman. "These criminals have us outnumbered. And it's almost time for lunch."

"Stop stalling!" growled the Dirty Bubble. "Surrender or fight. It's up to you."

"But hurry," Man Ray snarled. "It's almost time for lunch."

"I just said that," Mermaidman protested. Then he turned to Man Sponge and whispered, "How do you think we should handle these ruffians? Got any brilliant ideas?"

"Brilliant ideas are the only kind Man Sponge has!" Boy Patrick said enthusiastically.

Man Sponge smiled. "Thanks, Boy Patrick." Then he concentrated, using all the power of his tremendous brain. "Well," he said to Mermaidman, "you could use your utility belt."

"Excellent plan!" Mermaidman cried. He looked down at his belt. "Let's see. Which ray should I use? The Heat Ray? The Cold Ray? The Tanning Ray?"

"I don't think tanning the bad guys is going to help," Barnacleboy said.

"How about the Blast Ray?" Man Sponge suggested.

"And quickly!" Boy Patrick added. The villains were closing in.

"You got it, Bucky!" Mermaidman said. He pressed a button on his belt.

WHAM!

A shock wave blasted out around the heroes. It left the good guys unharmed, but knocked the bad guys far, far away.

"That's the ticket!" Barnacleboy shouted, clapping his hands with glee.

"Thank you, Man Sponge!" Mermaidman said, shaking his hand. "We couldn't have done it without you! If anyone deserves to borrow this belt anytime they want, it's you!"

At least, that's the way I remember it, SpongeBob thought as his mind returned to the present. "Well, I guess I should return the belt."

He started to walk in the direction Mermaidman and Barnacleboy had driven. Suddenly, he had a change of heart. He turned on his heel and sprinted back to the Krusty Krab!

Wearing the belt, he slammed the kitchen door and leaned up against it. "Or maybe not!" he said, giggling mischievously.

"I could just hold on to it until after work," he said, talking himself into it.

SpongeBob looked down at the belt fastened around his square pants. "All alone with Mermaidman's belt. . . . I wonder what this button does?"

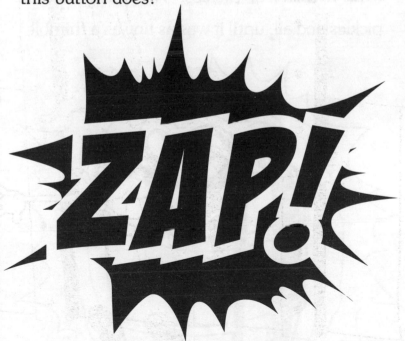

WHALE OF A TALE

A beam of strange light came out of the belt. It hit a barrel of pickles. The barrel shrank, pickles and all, until it was as tiny as a thimble!

SpongeBob balanced the barrel of pickles on the end of his finger. "Wow," he marvelled. "The Small Ray!"

He remembered one time when Mermaidman had used the Small Ray. . . .

Man Sponge and Boy Patrick were finishing up another day of keeping Bikini Bottom safe when Mermaidman and Barnacleboy drove up in the Invisible Boatmobile.

"Man Sponge! Come quickly! There's a new villain in town and we need your help!" Mermaidman said.

Man Sponge and Boy Patrick hopped in the backseat. They roared off, heading toward City Hall.

When they got there, they ran into the mayor's office. The mayor had been tied up. Sitting in his chair was the biggest fish that Man Sponge had ever seen!

Mermaidman pointed an accusing finger at the huge fish. "Get out of the mayor's chair immediately!" he ordered.

The gigantic fish chuckled a low, menacing laugh. Then he stood up. His head grazed the ceiling. "You listen to me, pal. I'm Whale Shark, and I'm the biggest fish in the sea! That means, what I say goes."

"Not if I have anything to say about it!"

Mermaidman said bravely.

Whale Shark took one step and loomed over Mermaidman. "Oh, yeah?" he asked. "And what exactly do you have to say about it, little man?"

Mermaidman gulped. "Well, I haven't exactly had time to put my thoughts in order. I'm really better with a prepared speech. . . ."

Things looked bad for Mermaidman

and Barnacleboy. Just as Whale Shark was about to attack them, Man Sponge shouted, "Mermaidman! Your belt! THE SMALL RAY!"

"Oh, yeah!" Mermaidman cried. He punched a button on his belt.

ZZZAAAAAAP!!

The strange beam hit Whale Shark, making him glow for a second. Then he shrank down to the size of a sea nut! "Hey!" he squeaked. "What'd you do to me?!"

"Yay!" Boy Patrick cheered, picking up Whale Shark with no problem.

Mermaidman turned to Man Sponge. "Thanks, Man Sponge! We couldn't have done it without you!"

Man Sponge blushed modestly. "Oh, it was nothing, really. . . ."

At least, that was the way SpongeBob
remembered it.

He couldn't resist playing with the Small Ray, and soon he had created a tiny Krusty Krab kitchen with things that he'd shrunk!

Squidward heard all the zapping and laughing and came into the kitchen to investigate. "SpongeBob, what's going on in here?" he asked.

Squidward stared at all the things SpongeBob had shrunk. His hat, his spatula—even a miniature Krabby Patty for a bug to eat at a little table!

"Why's everything
so tiny?" Squidward
asked suspiciously.

"I don't know,"
SpongeBob replied
sheepishly, trying to
hide the belt behind his
back.

"What have you got there?"
Squidward asked.

"Nothing!"

"No really,
let's see it!"
Then he gasped.
"Is that Mermaidman's
belt?!"

"Yes." SpongeBob's
teeth chattered with
nerves.

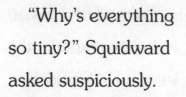

"Wow, I find it hard to believe he'd lend it to you!" Squidward remarked.

"Me . . . either . . . hee, hee," SpongeBob let out.

Squidward gasped with disbelief when the truth finally sank in. "He didn't lend it to you . . . did he?"

SQUIDWARD'S REVENGE

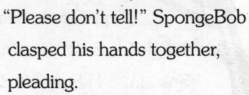

"Please don't tell!" SpongeBob clasped his hands together, pleading.

Squidward pointed at SpongeBob accusingly. "You STOLE it!"

"PLEASE DON'T TELL!"

SpongeBob begged.

"Oh, I'm telling," Squidward said, nodding. This was the perfect opportunity to get back at SpongeBob for driving him crazy every day at work.

"Squidward," SpongeBob said desperately. "If Mermaidman finds out, he'll kick me out of his fan club for sure. Please don't tell!"

Squidward pointed his thumb over his shoulder at the phone hanging on the kitchen wall. "Uh-oh," he said. "There's the phone!"

SpongeBob clutched his head frantically. "NO!"

Squidward started backing toward the wall.

51

"I'm walking toward the phone. . . ."

"NO!!!" SpongeBob screamed, reaching out toward Squidward.

"I'm getting closer to the phone," Squidward said. He thoroughly enjoyed toying with SpongeBob. He stretched one tentacle toward the phone. . . .

"NOOOO!" SpongeBob sobbed.

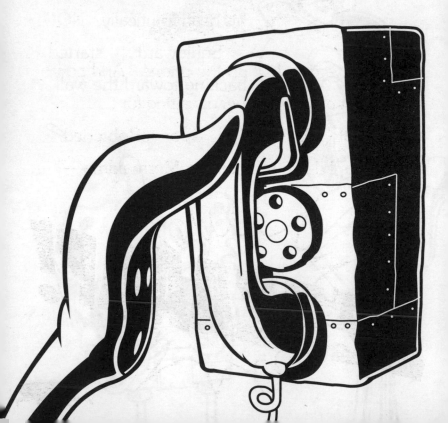

Squidward picked up the phone. "And now,
the moment we've all been waiting for . . ."

"I'M BEGGING YOU!" SpongeBob cried.

"Hello, I'd like to speak to Mermaidma—"

ZZZZAAAP!

ZAP!

PART II

Squidward dropped the phone's receiver as he flew up in the air and landed on a chopping block next to a knife and a tomato. He was tiny! "What did you do to me?!" he cried.

The phone bonked Squidward on the head as it fell down. He could hear Mermaidman saying, "Hello? Hello?"

SpongeBob hung up the phone and said sadly, "I'm sorry, Squidward, but you made me do it."

Squidward pointed his tentacle at SpongeBob angrily. "SpongeBob, if you don't return me to normal size RIGHT NOW, you are gonna be in really big trouble!"

SpongeBob grasped Mermaidman's belt nervously. "Uh, okay. Uh . . ." He had no idea how to unshrink Squidward!

"I said now!" Squidward yelled.

"Uh . . . ," SpongeBob said, staring down at the controls on the belt. There were buttons of all shapes, colours, and sizes. There were complicated switches and dials . . . and he had no idea what any of them did!

"DO YOU HEAR ME?!" Squidward shouted as loud as he could.

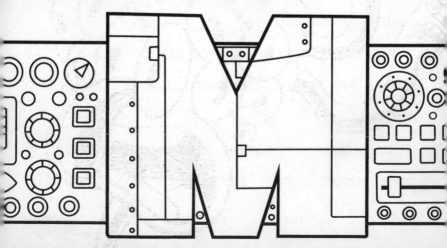

Holding his breath, SpongeBob pushed a button. He hoped it would return Squidward to his normal size.

ZZZZAAAAAPP!!

"YAAHHH!" Squidward shrieked. He looked like he had a hundred eyes, and there were tiny snakes growing out of his head!

"Holy fish paste! Get it off me!" he screeched. "Get it off me!" Squidward grabbed the clump of eyes and snakes and tossed it away.

He was breathing hard. "Don't you know how to work that thing?" he gasped.

SpongeBob tried to look confident. "Uh, I can do it," he claimed uncertainly. He picked another button and pressed it.

ZAP!

Squidward's nose grew until it was the size of his whole body!

ZAAAAP!

His nose shrank, but now his feet were huge!

ZZAP!

His feet shrank, but now he was freezing cold!

ZAPP!

Now he was burning hot!

ZAAP!

Now he started whirling around like a tornado!

ZZZAAAAAPP!!

Now he couldn't stop dancing wildly!

ZZZZAAP!

Now he looked
like he was made
out of mud!

ZAPP!!

Now he looked like he was made out of stone!

ZAAAP!

Squidward stood on the chopping block with smoke rising from his skin. He was still tiny!

"STOP!" he screamed. All these changes were extremely uncomfortable, and none of them were getting Squidward back to his normal size.

"I've got an idea!" Squidward said. "Let's call Mermaidman and—"

"NO!" SpongeBob cried. He grabbed Squidward and picked him up. "I can't let you do that!"

SpongeBob thought hard. What should he do? He couldn't leave Squidward tiny, but he couldn't get kicked out of Mermaidman's fan club.

"There must be someone else who can help," he said. "Someone smart and wise with years of life experience . . ."

OH, PICKLE!

Patrick was leaning on his rock house, waiting for SpongeBob to come home from the Krusty Krab. He was looking forward to being Boy Patrick again.

SpongeBob ran up, waving his hands. "Patrick! Patrick!" he called frantically.

"Man Sponge!" Patrick answered. "Boy Patrick is ready for action!"

But SpongeBob didn't have time to *play* superhero. He had a *real* superhero problem to solve! The words tumbled out as he nervously explained, "Patrick, I was at work,

and Mermaidman and Barnacleboy came,
and then I got this belt, and look!"

He reached in his pocket and pulled out
Squidward, who was still very, very small. He
held him up for Patrick to see.

Patrick was excited. "A Squidward action
figure!" he gasped. "Let me play with him!"

Before SpongeBob could explain that the little figure was the *real* Squidward, Patrick snatched him out of SpongeBob's hand. "Fighter pilot!" he exclaimed, delighted with the new "toy."

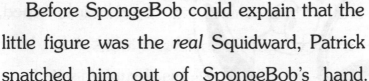

He moved Squidward around, back and forth, up and down, as though he were zooming through the air in a jet. "Dive bomb!" Patrick shouted.

Squidward yelped,
but Patrick didn't hear
his shrunken voice.

"Let's see how far I
can throw it!" Patrick
dared.

"Patrick, no!" SpongeBob
yelled, putting out his hands to stop him.
"That's not an action figure! That's the real
Squidward. I shrank him by accident."

"Ohhh," Patrick said, holding Squidward
still. Then he cocked his arm, ready to toss
a forward pass. "Let's
see how far I can
throw him!"

Squidward
screamed. SpongeBob
stopped Patrick again.

"Wait! You don't

understand! This is serious. I don't know how to unshrink him. He could be stuck like this for the rest of his life."

SpongeBob looked really worried. Patrick tried to reassure him.

"Aw, don't worry about it," Patrick said. "He'll find love one day."

"You think so?" SpongeBob asked.

"Sure!" Patrick said confidently. "But it'll be with someone his own size. Like this pickle!"

Patrick held up a pickle. Sure enough, it was just about the same size as shrunken Squidward.

"See?" Patrick said happily. "They like each other!"

Squidward frowned at the pickle. Patrick started to move the pickle toward Squidward.

"No, no, no, no . . . !" he said.

But Patrick couldn't hear Squidward's tiny voice. He pushed the pickle right

into Squidward's face, making kissing sounds. "Mwah! Mwah! Mwah!"

"Bleah!" Squidward grunted.

SpongeBob sighed and looked down at Mermaidman's belt. "If only I knew how to work this thing," he said.

Patrick got excited. "You know what?" he asked. "This is just like one of my favourite episodes of *The Adventures of Mermaidman and Barnacleboy*! And lucky for you," Patrick said proudly, "I remember exactly how it went!"

WUMBORAMA

"Mermaidman was talking to his friend, Barnacleguy—," Patrick said.

"Barnacleboy," SpongeBob corrected.

Patrick struck a very dramatic pose. "Mermaidman screamed, 'I sense WEEVILS!'"

"I think you mean 'evil,'" SpongeBob said.

Patrick broke out of his pose. "Who's telling this story? You or me?"

"Sorry," SpongeBob said.

"So Mermaidman and Barnacleboy ran to Boy Patrick for help," Patrick continued. "They needed him to help fight the scary weevils."

SpongeBob didn't remember this episode at all.

"Boy Patrick said, 'Don't worry! I will help you! I'm not afraid of ANYTHING!' So they jumped into the Inedible Boatmobile. . . ."

SpongeBob started to say something, but Patrick waved him off and kept telling his story.

"And drove to downtown Bikini Bottom, where the giant weevils were eating the buildings and then burping. And the burps smelled horrible. Like this."

Patrick gave a tremendous belch. Squidward looked sick.

"So Mermaidguy and Barnacledude turned

to Boy Patrick and screamed, 'Boy Patrick! What should we do?!'"

Patrick jumped up and down and waved his arms, acting out the story.

"And Boy Patrick thought really hard and then he said, 'Why don't you use your secret utility belt?' And so they did, and it worked, and Boy Patrick was a hero. The end."

At least that was the way Patrick remembered it. He crossed his arms and looked smug.

SpongeBob was puzzled. "That's a great story, Patrick. But what does it have to do with getting Squidward back to his normal size?"

"It proves," Patrick said patiently, "that I know all about Mermaidman's belt. Here, let me take a closer look."

Patrick leaned down and stared at the belt for

about a second. "Hmmm," he said, rubbing his chin. "You know what the problem is?"

"What?" asked SpongeBob eagerly.

"You've got it set on *M* for 'mini' when it should be set on *W* for 'wumbo'!" Patrick announced triumphantly. He grabbed the *M* belt buckle and turned it upside down so it looked like a *W*.

SpongeBob frowned. "Patrick, I don't think 'wumbo' is a real word."

Patrick just shook his head.

"Come on! You know, I wumbo; you wumbo; he, she, me wumbo. . . ."

Patrick still tightly clutched Squidward. He rolled his eyes as Patrick kept explaining.

"Wumboing, will have be wumbo? Wumborama? Wumbology, the study of wumbo? This is stuff you learn in first grade, SpongeBob!"

SpongeBob smiled. "Patrick, I'm sorry I doubted you."

"All right then," Patrick said. "Let her rip!"

zZZZZAAAAAP!!

ZAP!

PART III

Patrick looked at Squidward. They were both the same size! "Yay!" Patrick cheered. "It worked!"

"Oh no!" SpongeBob cried. He reached down and picked up Patrick *and* Squidward.

Patrick pointed at SpongeBob. "Look! SpongeBob's giant! Can I be giant next?"

"Patrick, I'm not giant," SpongeBob explained. "You've shrunk too!"

Patrick was the same size as Squidward because the Small Ray had shrunk him! Now SpongeBob had *two* shrunken friends to worry about!

"You're kidding!" Patrick said, surprised. He reached in his pocket and pulled out the pickle he'd shoved into Squidward's face. "Good thing I've still got this pickle."

Patrick started kissing the pickle. "Mwah! Mwah! Mmmmwah!"

"HEY!" Squidward yelled to get SpongeBob's attention. "NOW will you take us to Mermaidman?"

SpongeBob looked horrified. "NO!" he yelped. "He must never find out!"

Squidward reeled back from being yelled at by someone so much bigger than him.

SpongeBob looked sorry. "But I'll think of something," he said. "I promise!"

He pulled a jar out of his pocket. "Until then, you'll be safe in this jar." He dropped Squidward and Patrick into the jar.

Patrick turned to Squidward. "You know what's funny? My pickle started out in a jar, and now it's in one again!" He shrugged. "Huh. It's like a pun or something." Patrick laughed, but Squidward was not amused.

SpongeBob was sweating nervously. He tried to reassure himself. "It's only two people. No big deal. Nobody saw it."

Just then Sandy walked up, startling SpongeBob.

"Howdy, SpongeBob!"

Without even thinking, SpongeBob had whirled around and zapped Sandy with the Small Ray! Now she was tiny too!

"What did y'all do to me?" she asked, astonished to be so small.

"I'm sorry, Sandy!" SpongeBob cried. He tried to explain the whole mess as he put Sandy in his jar too. "You see,

Mermaidman came into the Krusty Krab and—"

Just then Larry the Lobster walked up behind SpongeBob, startling him again.

"Hey, SpongeBob!" Larry said.

ZZAAAAAAAPPPP!!!

SpongeBob screamed and caught the shrunken lobster in his jar.

Then another fish walked up and greeted SpongeBob.

ZZAAAPPR!

Then a girl fish.

ZZAAAAPPPP!!!

Then Mrs. Puff.

ZZAAAAPPPP!!!

Then Scooter, the surfer fish.

85

ZZAAAAAAAAPPPP!!!

Everywhere he went, SpongeBob bumped into more people who knew him. They all got shrunk and caught in the jar!

Soon he'd walked all the way downtown. He squeezed the lid onto his jar. "I'm going to have to get a bigger jar," he said.

SpongeBob looked around the deserted streets. He was all alone. He'd shrunk everyone in Bikini Bottom!

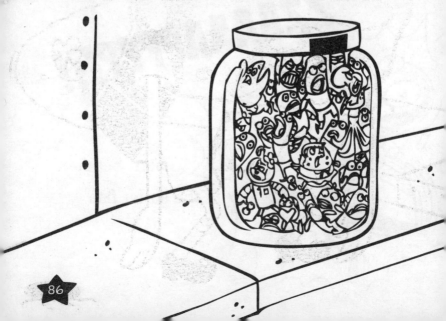

FISH JAR

Inside the jar, Squidward was pressed up against so many people. "SpongeBob, will you just face the facts?" he snarled. "You've got to go to Mermaidman!"

"Oh, Squidward," SpongeBob said, starting to sniffle. "He'll be so disappointed."

From inside the jar, Sandy snapped, "Well, you can't leave us small forever!"

SpongeBob fell to his knees and sobbed. "You don't understand!" he wailed.

But then a comforting voice said, "SpongeBob, you need to admit your mistake."

SpongeBob looked closely at the jar to see who had spoken. "Mum?" he asked as he wiped tears away from his eyes.

Then another voice spoke from inside the jar. "Your mother's right, son. Mermaidman will understand."

Barnacleboy turned to the speaker. "*You're* Mermaidman, you old coot!"

"Ohh, yeah," Mermaidman said.

He'd been shrunk and placed in the jar too!

SpongeBob turned the jar until he found his favourite superhero. "Mermaidman?" he said. "I'm so sorry! It's just that I'm such a big fan. And your belt—"

"Aw, don't worry, son," Mermaidman said reassuringly. "I understand. Why, I remember back when I first used the belt. The year was nineteen aught eleventy-twelve. I believe the president then was—"

"JUST TELL HIM HOW TO UNSHRINK US!" everyone else in the jar shouted.

"Oh, uh, yes, the Unshrink Ray!" Mermaidman said, thinking hard. "Let's see, uh, um . . . did you set it to wumbo?"

The jarful of angry citizens couldn't believe their ears. "WHAT?!" they roared.

SpongeBob was holding the packed jar in his hands. It started to vibrate, then shake violently. He could barely hold on to it!

Then . . .

WHOOOOOOOOOSH!

It was too packed to hold everyone, and all of the shrunken people of Bikini Bottom came shooting out of the jar like a geyser! They flew up into the air and landed on the ground near SpongeBob.

The mob of tiny sea-dwellers formed themselves into words that made up a sentence. SpongeBob read the sentence out loud. . . .

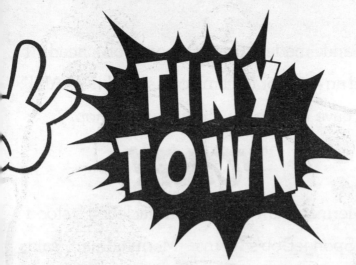

TINY TOWN

The furious Bikini Bottomites rushed toward SpongeBob's shoes and climbed up his legs and started kicking!

Squidward quickly found his way up to SpongeBob's stomach. "Now I have to drive five miles to go to the bathroom . . . in my own home!"

He kicked SpongeBob's stomach.

OOOOOFF!

Sandy made it up to SpongeBob's head. "I need an elevator to climb one stair! HI-YAAH!" She gave his head a sharp karate chop.

YOUCH!

Mermaidman and Barnacleboy stood on SpongeBob's arms. Mermaidman said, "We've been shrinking for years . . ."

"But this is ridiculous!" Barnacleboy added. Caught up in the anger of the mob, they kicked SpongeBob too.

YEECH!

Angry fish were attacking every part of SpongeBob's giant body. He was knocked into every possible shape and weird position.

He clutched his head and saw stars. Then he heard the crowd shout something. . . .

"EVERYTHING'S TOO BIG!"

Suddenly, that gave SpongeBob an idea! He raised his index finger and said, "I've got it!"

From inside SpongeBob, Squidward and the others heard a familiar

ZZZZZZAAAAAPP!!

Then they heard SpongeBob say, "Ta-da!"

They were eager to see what he'd shrunk this time and amazed when they realized that he hadn't shrunk *anyone*—he'd shrunk all the buildings in Bikini Bottom!

"Since I couldn't make you big," he explained, "I made the city small!"

The citizens poured out onto the streets to inspect their newly shrunken town.

"And now, only one more thing to shrink,"
SpongeBob said, lifting the buckle off
Mermaidman's belt. He pointed it at himself
like a camera. "Cheese!"

ZAP!

SpongeBob shrank down to everyone else's size.

Squidward looked around. "I guess this is okay," he said.

"Yeah!" Larry the Lobster agreed. "What's the difference?"

"Good job, SpongeBob!" another fish said. They all cheered!

"Another brilliant idea, Man Sponge!" Patrick shook SpongeBob's hand.

"Thanks, Boy Patrick!" SpongeBob said, grinning.

As everyone celebrated SpongeBob's clever solution, a full-size bus pulled up. Plankton got off the bus, carrying two suitcases. "Well, it's great to be back!"

Then he noticed the tiny city of Bikini Bottom. Standing next to it, he looked like a giant.

"Huh?" he said.

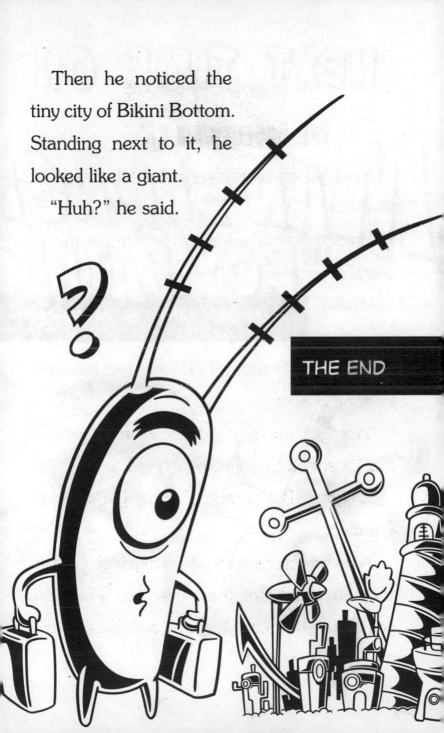

THE END

DUTY CALLS

SpongeBob pounded on Patrick's rock. "Patrick! Come on! It's time!"

His buddy's house flipped open with Patrick attached. He looked sleepy. "Time for what?" he mumbled. "A nap?"

"No!" SpongeBob said, shaking his head. "Time for us to visit . . . THE MERMALAIR!"

Patrick looked excited. "Oh yeah!" He hopped down and slammed his house shut. "I remember everything now! Except for two things: What's the Mermalair and why are we going there?"

As they hurried along the sidewalk together, SpongeBob reminded Patrick that the Mermalair was the supersecret headquarters of Bikini Bottom's boldest (and oldest) superheroes: Mermaidman and his faithful sidekick, Barnacleboy!

"They're going on holiday to Leisure Village," SpongeBob explained. "And while they're gone, you and I get to take care of the Mermalair!"

Patrick stopped in his tracks. "That sounds like an awfully big job," he said. "Too big for you and me."

SpongeBob nodded. "You might be right, Patrick." He rubbed his chin, thinking hard. Then he snapped his fingers. "But it's not too big of a job for . . .

MAN SPONGE AND BOY PATRICK!